Sister for Sale is dedicated to my precious
daughters, Abby and Allyson—my daily inspiration.
— M.M.A.

For Connor and Holly
— K.S.B.

Written by Michelle Medlock Adams

Illustrated by Karen Stormer Brooks

Zonderkidz

Dear God, I need your help today.
I'm writin' me an ad.

How do you spell, "Sister For Sale?"
I need to know real bad.

Can I tell you all about her?
Please tell me what you'd say.

I've got her running through my head.
She's been in there all day.

Okay, here goes:

Sister For Sale—a real bargain for you!
She's worth about a hundred bucks,
but I'll sell her for two.

Her name is
Allyson Michelle.

She's just a
little mean.

She's not real good.

She's not real bad.

She's somewhere
in between.

She has blonde hair and big, blue eyes and freckles on her nose.
Not long ago she cut her hair!
But that's okay, it grows.

She blames me for her wiggly tooth.
She says I made her fall.

But that's a lie.
She made it up!
That's not the truth at all!

She doesn't share her toys with me,

and sometimes she takes mine.

But if you buy her
I'm quite sure,

she'll share with you
just fine.

I need to tell you something else.
She snores a lot at night.

And if she doesn't get her way,
she has been known to bite.

But hey! Nobody's perfect, right?
She's still an awesome buy!

I might sell her for just one buck,
if you think two's too high.

She's funny and
she's sort of smart.

She rides her bike
real good.

In fact, some days
I like my sis.

I'd keep her if
I could.

I might miss her if she were gone.
There'd be nothin' to do.

You made her and you love her, God.
I guess I'll love her too.

I guess she isn't all that bad.
Sometimes, she's kinda fun.

For you, I'll keep her after all,
'cause she's my only one.

Mom's Moment

Sibling loyalty grows best in a home where everyone knows that God gives us each other so that we may learn how to love . . . in spite of all our good and not-so-good parts . . . because that's how he loves us.

Sister For Sale
Text copyright © 2002 by Michelle Medlock Adams
Illustrations copyright © 2002 by Karen Stormer Brooks

Requests for information should be addressed to:

Zonderkidz

The children's group of Zondervan
Grand Rapids, MI 49530
www.zonderkidz.com

Zonderkidz is a trademark of Zondervan.

ISBN 0-310-70254-2

Art direction and design by Jody Langley

Printed in China
02 03 04 05 / HK / 5 4 3 2 1